Wide Range Readers

Phyllis Flowerdew

Oliver & Boyd

Illustrated by John Harrold

OLIVER & BOYD
Robert Stevenson House
1–3 Baxter's Place
Leith Walk
Edinburgh EH1 3BB
A Division of Longman Group Ltd

First published 1979
Fourth impression 1982

ISBN 0 05 003188 0

Printed in Hong Kong
by Sheck Wah Tong Printing Press Ltd

Preface

There are six Wide Range Readers Red Books. They can be used alone or with Wide Range Readers Blue and Green, with which they are parallel. The controlled vocabulary and graded sentence structure make them suitable for children with the following reading ages:—

7 to 7½ years	— Book 1
7½ to 8 years	— Book 2
8 to 8½ years	— Book 3
8½ to 9 years	— Book 4
9 to 10 years	— Book 5
10 to 11 + years	— Book 6

The success of Wide Range Blue and Green Books has been proved through the years, and the author hopes that the addition of the Red series will bring pleasure to teachers and children.

Where to Find the Stories

Ragabones Rabbit and the Honey Pot

"Rags and bones!" shouted Ragabones
Rabbit. "Any rags and bones?"

He pushed his little cart through the
woods. He had called at the farm on his
way. The farm dog had given him an old
bit of blanket from his kennel, and
three dry bones that he could not use
any more.

On the cart too, was a box of small
fluffy balls made of wool.

" I'm giving a woollen ball to anyone who brings me rags and bones today," said Ragabones Rabbit to the little animals who came up to him.

At once they ran off to their homes to see what they could find to give Ragabones Rabbit.

Soon they were back again, passing their bundles to him and saying, " Thank you ", as he gave them each a fluffy ball made of wool.

Little Badger had a ball.

Little Hedgehog had a ball.

Little Field Mouse had a ball, but Little Squirrel was still at home looking for something to give.

" I'm afraid we haven't anything today," said his mother, " except that empty honey pot those people left after their picnic. It's lying under the bushes over there."

" Yes. I'll take that," cried Little Squirrel. He pulled out the honey pot.

It was only a small one, and it still
had some stale and sticky honey left
at the bottom of it.

He ran through the woods with it
to Ragabones Rabbit, who was just about
to go.

"Ragabones Rabbit," panted Little
Squirrel, "I have something for you.
A honey pot."

"Thank you," replied Ragabones Rabbit.
"I can always sell jam jars and honey
pots to the jam factories. Bit sticky,
I see, but I'll wash it when I get home."

He put it on the cart, under the old
blanket from the farm dog's kennel, and
he handed Little Squirrel a small
fluffy ball made of wool.

" Thank you, Ragabones Rabbit," said
Little Squirrel.
He was so pleased that he threw it up
and caught it three times. Then he held
it tightly in his paw and climbed up
into a tree.

For a few minutes he watched Ragabones
Rabbit walking away with his cart, now
piled high with rags and bones.
Then suddenly Robin flew past, and said
in a worried voice.

" Hurry home Little Squirrel. Bad Fox
is about." Little Squirrel's heart
jumped with fear.

" Where ? " he asked, but Robin had already flown away.

Then Little Squirrel looked down and he saw Bad Fox creeping through the bushes, and hiding among the trees.
He saw him creeping, creeping after Ragabones Rabbit.
Little Squirrel shivered from the top of his head to the end of his tail.

" What shall I do ? " he thought. " How can I warn Ragabones Rabbit ? "
He was afraid to jump down and run after him. He was afraid to call out to him.
What *could* he do ?

For a while he did nothing except follow Ragabones Rabbit and Bad Fox. He followed by jumping from the top of one tall tree to another, so that no one knew that he was anywhere about.

So the three animals went on through the wood. Ragabones Rabbit pushed his little cart along the rough path. Bad Fox went creeping, creeping after him; and Little Squirrel went jumping from tree to tree after them both.

Someone else went following on too. It was a wasp, a striped, yellow wasp who could smell honey somewhere around. He buzzed a honey-call to his friends, and all the wild wasps of the wood came swarming after *him*.

So everyone went on through the wood. Ragabones Rabbit walked. Bad Fox crept. Little Squirrel jumped. The wild wasps flew; and Ragabones Rabbit was the only one who thought himself to be alone.

The first to catch up with Ragabones Rabbit were the wasps. He did not see them all, but he did notice a few buzzing around his cart.

" They're after that stale honey," he said to himself. He did not know that all the wild wasps of the woods were now creeping in and out among the rags and bones on his cart. They were going in and out of the honey pot, eating the honey.

The next to catch up with Ragabones Rabbit was Little Squirrel. He was now in the trees right over his head.

" If only Ragabones Rabbit would look up," thought Little Squirrel, " I could warn him quietly about Bad Fox."

But Ragabones Rabbit did *not* look up.
Little Squirrel could see that Bad Fox
was now getting very near indeed.

Nearer, nearer crept Bad Fox, nearer,
nearer. At any moment he would pounce on
poor Ragabones Rabbit. If Little
Squirrel were going to do anything
to help, he must do it *now*.

Suddenly he thought of his small,
fluffy ball made of wool.

" I'll throw it down," he said.
" Then Ragabones Rabbit will look up and
see me." Carefully he threw.
The ball landed right at Ragabones
Rabbit's feet. Still Ragabones Rabbit
did not look up. He looked down.
He stood still. He saw the ball roll
under his cart. He dived down to get
it.

" This," thought Bad Fox, " gives me a
good chance to catch him."
He stood quietly by the cart, waiting
for him to scramble to his feet again.

Now by this time, the wasps were getting angry. There was not room in the pot for them all. They were buzzing and buzzing, and just as Bad Fox stood by the cart, they all came swarming angrily out. They settled on the first animal they saw.

It happened to be Bad Fox. They stung his head, his neck, his paws. They buzzed angrily and stung him through his fur.

" Help ! Help ! " cried Bad Fox, and he rushed away, trying to brush off the angry, stinging wasps. He ran and ran with all the wild wasps of the wood following, and he did not stop until he reached his own den.

Then of course, Little Squirrel jumped down and told the surprised Ragabones Rabbit all that had happened.

" Thank you, thank you Little Squirrel for helping me," said Ragabones Rabbit, and he handed him back his small, fluffy ball.

" I think the wasps helped you more than I did," replied Little Squirrel. Then he said goodbye, and ran quickly home to show his mother the small, fluffy ball of wool.

As for Ragabones Rabbit, he hurried home too, and the first thing he did was to wash out the honey pot and rub it dry with a pawful of grass.

Gossamer

Little baby spiders
   Sailing on the air,
Leave their strings of gossamer
   Lying everywhere,
Tangled in the bushes,
   Trailing on the grass,
Floating through the autumn mist
   To touch you as you pass.

The Lighthouse

Once upon a time
there was a lighthouse.
It stood on the grassy cliffs
above the town, and it looked out across
the yellow sands and the cold, grey sea.
It was a white lighthouse, with a little
garden round it, and every night its
great, golden light flashed out over the
sea—one, two, flash ! One, two, flash !
One, two, flash !

The lighthouse man lived there with his wife and his big, tabby cat. He looked after the light, and kept its windows shining and clear.

Now cars keep to special roads on the land, and ships keep to special ways on the sea. Sometimes new roads are made on the land, and sometimes ways on the sea change too. As the years went by, that was just what happened.

Ships began to go a different way, and the lighthouse was not needed any more. Its great golden light flashed out over the sea for the last time. One, two, flash! One, two, flash! One, two, flash!

Next day the lighthouse man and his wife and his big tabby cat moved away, and the lighthouse was left empty. A notice was put up beside it, saying, " For Sale." It was empty for weeks and months, for who would want to buy a lighthouse?

Its windows became misty, and its
white paint began to peel.
Strong sea-grass and sea-thistles began
to spread over the little garden.
No one bought the lighthouse. No one
seemed to want it.

Now in the town lived four little
children with their mother and father.
The children were called Susan and Sally
and Terry and Tim. They lived in a very
small flat, in a very crowded street.
The flat had a tiny bathroom and a tiny
kitchen, and one living room and one
bedroom.

18

That meant that Mother and Father and Susan and Sally and Terry and Tim all had to share the same bedroom, and there was hardly room to move about.

Father had worked hard and saved up for years and years and years, and now, at last, he had enough money to buy a house.

He went to the house agent's office in the town, and said,

" I want to buy a house, please."

" How many bedrooms do you want ? " asked the man in the office.

" Three, please. I want one for my wife and myself, and one for Susan and Sally, and one for Terry and Tim."

" That's not very easy to find," said the man. " That's the sort of house nearly everyone wants. I could sell you a big house with six bedrooms. I could sell you a little house with one or two bedrooms, but I cannot sell you a house with three bedrooms."

He wrote down Father's name and address, and said,

"Call again in a few weeks. Perhaps I may have something to offer you then."

Sadly, Father began walking out of the office.

"Of course," said the man, "the old lighthouse is still for sale. That has three bedrooms and it's very cheap indeed."

"Lighthouse!" replied Father crossly. "Who would want to live in a lighthouse?"

The weeks went by. Susan and Sally and Terry and Tim were growing bigger all the time, and the little flat seemed more crowded than ever.

"We must buy a house," said Mother.

"I'll try again," said Father. So the next day he went to the house agent's office again. It was Saturday, so this time Susan and Sally and Terry and Tim went along with him.

A different man was in the office
today.

"I want to buy a house, please,"
said Father.

"How many bedrooms do you want?"
asked the man.

"Three, please," replied Father.
"I want one for my wife and myself, one
for Susan and Sally, and one for Terry
and Tim."

"That's not very easy to find," said
the man. "That's the sort of house
nearly everyone wants. I could sell you

a big house with six bedrooms. I could sell you a little house with one or two bedrooms, but I cannot sell you a house with three bedrooms."

He looked up Father's name and address in his book, and said,

" Call again in a few weeks. Perhaps I'll have something to offer you by then."

Sadly Father started walking out of the office with Susan and Sally and Terry and Tim.

" Of course," said the man, " the old lighthouse is still for sale. That has three bedrooms, and it's very cheap indeed."

" Lighthouse ! " replied Father crossly. " Who would want to live in a lighthouse ? "

" I would," said Susan and Sally both together.

" It would be lovely," agreed Terry and Tim. " Oh Daddy, do buy the lighthouse." Father was so surprised that he only stared at the children.

" It's very nice inside," said the man. " It has a good large living room, and a small bathroom and kitchen. It has three bedrooms, one above the other. It's only a short walk out of town and up on the cliffs. Very good air up there."

" Oh please, Daddy," begged the children.

" I tell you what," said the man. " I'll call for you at your flat at two o'clock this afternoon. I'll drive you all to the lighthouse and show you over it. Then you can think about it."

" Oh do let's go, Daddy," begged the children.

" All right," agreed Father slowly. " There's no harm in that, but I can tell you we shall not buy the lighthouse. We will buy a proper house or none at all."

So that afternoon, the man from the house agent's office called at the flat

in a big, red car. He drove Mother,
Father and the four children out of the
town and up on the cliffs to the
lighthouse.

Then he took a key from his pocket,
and unlocked the door. He showed the
family all over the lighthouse. He
showed them the living room on the ground
floor. He showed them the small
bathroom and kitchen.

Then he led them up the narrow stairs
to the first bedroom. Then he took them
up again to the second bedroom, and up

again to the third. Then he took them to
the little room on the top, where the
lamp had always been. He rubbed the
window with his handkerchief, and said,

" There's no one in town with a view
like that ! "

Mother, Father and the four children
looked out in wonder across the yellow
sands and the cold, grey sea. At that
moment the sun came out from behind a

cloud. It shone down on the water and turned it all to sparkling silver.

" Oh, it's beautiful ! " they whispered.

So, of course, Father bought the lighthouse, and a few weeks later the family moved in. Mother and Father slept in the first bedroom. Susan and Sally had the one above. Terry and Tim had the one above that.

They were all as pleased as could be, and even Father agreed that it was the nicest house he could possibly have bought.

How High ?

As high as a house
To a mouse,
As high as a pole
To a mole,
As high as a tree
To a bee,
Is a mountain
To me.
So high is a mountain
To me.

The Water of Life

Once upon a time there was a king
who had three sons.
One day the king became ill.
Many doctors came to see him, but none
of them could make him better.

Then there came a very old doctor
who was much wiser than the others.

" There is only one thing that will
cure the king," he said. " It is the
water of life."

" Where is it to be found ? " asked the king's sons.

" It is in a well on top of a high mountain in the north,"
replied the doctor.

" I will go and get some," said the eldest son. So he took some food and drink, and he took a skin bag to fill with the water of life.

He walked and walked, always to the north, until at last he came to the high mountain. He saw a path leading upwards, and beside the path sat an old man.

" What do you want ? " asked the old man.

" I am looking for the water of life," replied the eldest son. " My father is ill, and only the water of life will make him better."

" It is a hard climb up the mountain," said the old man, " and there is danger on the way. I have sat here every day for years and years. I have seen many people go up but I have never seen anyone come down."

" Can you give me any advice ? " asked the eldest son.

" Yes," said the old man. " Just follow the path. You will see a lot of big stones on the grass at the side.
Do not look straight at them.
Do not touch them.
Do not speak to them."

" That should be easy," said the eldest son. " Why should I wish to look at stones ? Why should I wish to touch them or speak to them ? "

" You will hear the stones calling you," explained the old man. " They will say unkind things. They will shout at you. If you look at them or touch them or speak to them, you will turn into a stone yourself."

" Thank you," said the eldest son, and he set off up the path. He could see the stones on the grass at the side, but he did not look straight at them. He did not touch them. He did not speak to them.

Then he heard voices. The stones began to say unkind things to him. They began to shout at him.

" How dare you ? " he cried angrily, and he turned round to strike them with his stick.

At once he was turned into a stone.

A week passed and the eldest son did not return home. The king grew worse and worse.

Then the second son said,

" I will go and get some of the water

of life." So he took some food and drink and he took a skin bag to fill with the water of life.

He walked and walked, always to the north, until at last he came to the high mountain. He saw a path leading upwards, and beside the path he saw the old man.

" What do you want ? " asked the old man.

" I am looking for the water of life,"
replied the second son. " My father is
ill, and only the water of life will
make him better."

" It is a hard climb up the mountain,"
said the old man, " and there is danger
on the way. I have sat here every day
for years and years. I have seen many
people go up, but I have never seen
anyone come down."

" Can you give me any advice ? " asked
the second son.

" Yes," said the old man. " Just follow
the path. You will see a lot of big
stones on the grass at the side.
Do not look straight at them.
Do not touch them.
Do not speak to them."

" That should be easy," said the boy.
" Why should I wish to look at stones ?
Why should I wish to touch them or
speak to them ? "

" You will hear the stones calling you,"
explained the old man. " They will say
unkind things. They will shout at you.
If you look at them or touch them or
speak to them, you will turn into a
stone yourself."

" Thank you," said the boy, and he set
off up the path. He could see the stones
on the grass at the side, but he did not
look straight at them.
He did not touch them.
He did not speak to them.

Then he heard voices. The stones began
to say unkind things to him. They began
to shout at him. He did not answer.
He walked straight on.

Then he heard his brother's voice
calling, calling him.

" Where are you ? " answered the second
boy, and he swung round and stared at
the stones.

At once he was turned into a stone
himself.

A week passed, and the second son did not return home. The king grew worse and worse.

Then the third son said,

" I will go and get some of the water of life." So he took some food and drink and he took a skin bag to fill with the water of life.

He came at last to the high mountain just as his brothers had done. He spoke to the old man and listened to his advice. Then he set off up the path.

He could see the stones on the grass at the side, but he did not look straight at them. He did not touch them. He did not speak to them.

Then he heard voices. The stones began to say unkind things to him. They began to shout at him. He did not answer. He put his hands over his ears and he walked straight on.

He thought he heard his brothers' voices, but he pressed his hands more

tightly over his ears, and went on up
the path.

Soon there was no more grass at the
side of the path. There were no more
stones. There were only rocks.
Up and up climbed the boy.

Then at last he came to the top of
the mountain, and there was the well
filled with the water of life.

Gladly he filled his skin bag, and
started to climb down again. Down he
went, down and down until he came once
more to the grass and the stones.

He was trying so hard not to look straight at them, that he stumbled a little. A drop of water was shaken out of his bag. It fell on to a stone. The stone turned at once into a tall man.

" Thank you. Thank you," he said. "You have set me free."

Together they ran from stone to stone, splashing a few drops of water on every one. Each stone turned at once into a man or a woman or a boy or a girl.

In a little while the boy found his own brothers, and the three of them ran happily down the mountain together, followed by all the other people.

Then the brothers took back the rest of the water to their father the king. They poured it from the bag into a silver cup. The king drank eagerly, and at once he was cured.

Adapted from Favourite Stories
by Frank Francis (Collins)

The Windmill

It used to grind the farmer's corn
As its sails turned round and round,
But now it stands quite hushed and still,
For there's no more corn to be ground,
                              to be ground.
There's no more corn to be ground.

For streets were made and houses built
In the place where the corn once grew,
So the windmill stands quite hushed and still
And has nothing at all to do,
                              to do,
And has nothing at all to do.

The Branch Baby

Long, long ago there lived a little
cave girl, called Shell.
She had a brother called Reed, and they
lived with their mother and father
in a big, dry cave in the hillside.

There were other families living
near by, but all the children were older
than Shell.

" I wish I could have a friend
my own size," she often thought.

Sometimes she played with Reed,
but usually she played alone. She played
with something she called her baby.
It was just a small bit of a branch
but it looked as if it had a little face.

It had two little marks that looked
like eyes. It had a little knob that
looked like a nose. It had a little,
crooked line that looked like a mouth.

It had no legs, no arms, no hair,

but to Shell, it was a baby.
It must really have been one of the
very first dolls in the world.

Shell made a dress for it from a leaf.
She tied the leaf round its branch body
with a strong bit of grass.
She washed the baby. She nursed it.
She sang to it in her gruff, tuneless
little voice.

" A baby ? " said Reed sometimes,
teasing her. " It's just a bit of old
branch."

" No, it isn't," replied Shell.
" It has a little face and a green leaf
dress. Can't you see ? "

" It's a funny looking baby," said Reed.

One morning Shell and Reed went out
to look for berries. They swung and
jumped from tree to tree, not touching
the ground at all. Shell had her baby
tucked inside the top of her animal skin
dress.

The children were going to a patch
of low bushes where there were usually
a lot of berries. It was quite
a long way. Reed began to go too fast
for Shell. She found herself getting
left behind, and she tried to hurry.

She took a big jump. She almost fell,
and the branch baby was jerked up out of
her animal skin dress.
It fell down and down through the
branches of the tree. It fell somewhere
out of sight far, far below.

" Oh ! " cried Shell. " I've lost my baby ! "

She was afraid to climb down. She did
not know the way on the ground at all,
and she might get lost.

"Reed!" she called. "Wait for me!
Wait for me!" But Reed did not hear,
so there was nothing Shell could do
except hurry after him.

Soon Reed stopped and waited for her.
Then he saw that she was crying.

"I dropped my baby," she sobbed.
"We'll have to go back and look for it."

"Oh, you'll never find it," said Reed.
"I'll make you another one."

"I don't want another one," cried
Shell. "I want that one."

Reed was just going to say, " It's only
a bit of old branch," then he stopped,
for he knew that it was a baby to Shell.

" Do you know where you dropped it ? "
he asked.

" Yes. I know the tree. It was the one
with little curly leaves."

" Well, let's get the berries. Then
we'll look for the baby on the way back."
Shell did not feel too happy about it,
but she wiped away her tears and said,

" All right."

Soon the children had picked a lot of
berries. They wrapped them in leaves,
and tucked them inside the top of their
animal skin clothes. Then they set off
for home.

Soon they reached the tree with the
little curly leaves.

" Here's the tree," said Shell.

" All right. We'll climb down," said
Reed. " Keep close to me."

They dropped down from the lowest branch
and landed lightly on their feet.
They stood still and looked round.
The earth was dry and rocky and
rather bare.

" Can't see the baby," said Reed.

" It must be somewhere here," said
Shell. They walked up and down.
They looked and looked,
but they could not find the branch baby.

They looked behind stones.
They looked in the bushes, but they
could not find the branch baby.

" Are you sure it was this tree ? "
asked Reed.

" Quite sure," said Shell.
Then she stood suddenly still as if she
had been frozen to the spot.

" Look ! " she whispered.
Reed looked. There was a footprint.
It was a child's footprint.
It was the mark of a little short foot
and five little fat toes. It was about
the size of Shell's footprint, but it
was *not* hers.

" It must be yours," said Reed.
" No, it isn't mine. Mine's quite
different. There must be a little girl
like me living somewhere near here—
or a little boy."

" We'd better go home," said Reed.
He thought it would be wise to keep away
from strangers.

But Shell was following footprints,
little footprints, the size of her own.
There was one here, one there,

then another one and another, pointing on
through the trees.

Then a moment later she saw a little
girl the same size as herself. She was
playing alone among some rocks.
Shell was so excited that she could
hardly breathe. She was so shy that she
dared not move.

Then the little girl looked up and saw
her. She walked forward and held out
both her hands in greeting. She pointed
to herself and said,

" Jay."
Shell pointed to herself and said,

"Shell." Their speech was not quite
the same as each other's, but they smiled
and pointed and made signs, and
understood each other well enough.

Then Jay pulled aside some grass from
the back of a rock, and said,

"Look!" Shell looked.
She saw a branch baby about the size of
her own. It had little arms and legs
and it looked almost alive.

Someone had also chipped a little face
on it. It had two little chips for eyes.
It had one little chip for a nose.
It had a small slit, turning up at each
end, like a little smiling mouth. This
baby wore a fur dress, tied round its
body with a bit of grass.

" Baby ! " cried Shell in delight.
" A branch baby ! "

Then Jay pulled aside more grass from
the back of the rock, and held up
another baby. This one had on rather a
crumpled leaf dress. It was Shell's own
branch baby !

Jay tried to explain that it had fallen
from a tree.

" Oh ! " cried Shell. " It's mine !
I lost it."

" I was making a new dress for it,"
said Jay, and she held up a tiny bit of
animal fur, soft and silky and warm.

" You may have it," she added.

" Thank you," said Shell. She hugged
her baby and put the new fur dress on it,
and tied it with grass.
She was very happy.

Now all this time, Reed had waited in
the shadows of the trees.

" Shell," he called at last. " Come ! "

" Come and see me again," begged Jay.

" Oh yes," nodded Shell. Then she ran
back to Reed, holding the branch baby in
its new fur dress.

" I'm glad you found it," said Reed,
" though I don't know why you made such a
fuss about a bit of old branch."

Reed helped her to climb back up into
the trees, and Shell sang in her gruff,
tuneless little voice all the way home.

A Page of Riddles

Q. What makes a tree noisy ?
A. Its bark.

Q. What can never be made right ?
A. Your left ear.

Q. What looks like half a loaf of bread ?
A. The other half.

Q. Which word is always spelled wrongly ?
A. Wrongly.

Q. What will you get if you cross
   a sheep with a kangaroo ?
A. A woolly jumper.

Q. What can you make that no one can see ?
A. A noise.

The Witch's Cat

There was once a boy called Ivan
who lived with his father and his
grandmother near a great, dark forest
of fir trees.

Grandmother was very good at telling
stories. In the evenings, she and Ivan
would sit by the fire and wait for
Father to come home from work.
They would watch the big, black pot
that hung above the flames,
and Grandmother would tell stories.

But one evening, it was Ivan
who began the story.

"Grandmother," he said, "have you
heard the story about the witch who lives
in the forest with her cat?"

"What does she do?" asked Grandmother.

"They say she sends her cat to fetch
food for her. Is it true?"

"It could be," said Grandmother.
"Cats do sometimes hunt for birds and
small rabbits."

"But this cat doesn't bring back birds
or rabbits," said Ivan. "People say it
brings back children—little boys and
girls." His eyes grew wide with fear at
the very thought. Then he went on,

"And they say that if you run away
from it, it runs after you, and as it
runs it gets bigger and bigger. And the
more you run, the bigger it gets."

"That's what they say," said
Grandmother, "but they should have told
you something else too."

" What's that, Grandmother ? "

" They should have told you what happens
if you don't turn and run."

" Yes ? "

" If you are brave enough to stand still
and stare at the cat, it will not be able
to hurt you. If you go nearer to it,
it will get smaller. And if you go
nearer and nearer, it will get smaller
and smaller until it will disappear
altogether."

" Oh ! " whispered Ivan. He would have
asked more questions about the witch and
her cat, but just then Father came in.
Grandmother served the evening meal,
and they all talked of other things.

. . . . . .

A few weeks later, Ivan and some of
his friends went to the forest to gather
wood for the fires. They did this every
week. They usually picked up any small
twigs they could find. But now it was

getting near Christmas, and they were hoping to find some good logs.

Some of the boys had sledges to carry the wood home on. Ivan had a fine new sledge that Father had made for his birthday. It was painted like the holly trees—green and red, and it had a strong rope to pull it along.

The forest looked beautiful. The ground was white with snow; and snow was sparkling along the branches of the dark green fir trees.

" Let's go a bit further into the forest today," said one of the boys.

" Yes," agreed another. " We might find a big branch broken off by heavy snow."

Laughing and shouting and throwing snowballs at each other, they ran in and out among the trees.

Ivan's sledge glided swiftly behind him, jumping over bumps and stones as if it were alive. He ran on and on.

His cheeks grew pink in the cold, fresh air. He did not bother to pick up the smaller twigs he would usually take home. He wanted to find a really big log for the Christmas fire.

On and on he went, further and further into the forest. He did not notice that he was leaving the other boys far behind.

Then suddenly he found that he was all alone. He did not mind at first. He just went on looking for a big log. He went on looking and looking—and then an awful thought came to him. He thought of the witch and her cat. He tried to push it from his mind, but he could not.

He badly wanted his friends now, and he
called loudly.

"Hullo! Hullo!" But his voice blew
away on the wind, and no answer came
back to him.

At that moment a squirrel jumped in a
tree behind him. It sent a little pile
of snow tumbling down to earth. Ivan was
used to all the sounds of the forest,
but he did not think of squirrels just
then. He was so frightened that he began
to run.

" It might be the witch's cat," he thought.

He could not run very fast because the sledge often caught in small bushes or tree stumps. Once when it did this, he turned round to free it.

Something moved among the tree trunks. Ivan gave a little gasp of fear. He let go of the ropes, and left the sledge in the snow. He ran. He ran. It was easier without the sledge. Then he turned his head again.

There it was—the witch's cat—running, running, not far behind him. His heart beat so loudly that he could feel it knocking against his chest.

He forgot all that his grandmother had told him. The cat was only the size of the cats in the village, but Ivan ran away from it as fast as he could.

He turned his head to look at it. It was bigger now. It was as big as a dog.

Ivan ran and ran. He turned his head. The cat was as big as a wolf, and it was getting nearer, nearer.

Ivan ran and ran. He turned again. The cat was as big as a tiger, and it was getting nearer, nearer.

Ivan ran like the wind. His heart beat fast. His breath was coming in short gasps. He was getting tired. He could not run any faster. But he must! He must! The cat was as big as an elephant now, and it was close, close behind him.

Suddenly he thought of Grandmother.
He remembered her saying,

" If you are brave enough to stand still
and stare at the cat, it will not be able
to hurt you. If you go nearer to it, it
will get smaller."
Could he be brave enough to stand still
and stare at the cat ? Could he ?
Could he be brave enough ?
The cat was so near now. This might be
Ivan's last chance.

He stood still and turned round.
The cat stood still too.
It was as big as an elephant, but it
grew no bigger.

Ivan stared at it. It became a little
smaller.

Ivan grew brave. He stared harder.
The cat became smaller. It was tiger
size again, smooth and black, with eyes
like fires, but Ivan was getting braver
all the time. He stamped his foot and
said,

"Shoo! Go away!"
The cat turned round and took a step
away. Ivan took a step nearer to it.

The cat began to run. Ivan ran too.
He was no longer running away from the
witch's cat. He was running after it,
and it was growing smaller, smaller,
smaller.

Now it was the size of a wolf.

Now it was the size of a dog.

Now it was the size of the cats in
the village.

Now it was the size of a small rabbit.

Now it was the size of a mouse.

Ivan was no longer afraid. He ran and
ran after the cat.

Now it was a tiny, black little thing.
It was only the size of a beetle.

Now it was the size of a ladybird.

Now it was the size of an ant.

Now it was so small, he could hardly
see it.

Then suddenly Ivan stood still again.
There in front of him was the witch's
cottage, and in the doorway was the old
witch, looking out for her cat.

It was a shabby, dirty cottage
that looked as if it were about to
tumble down. It had thick, black smoke
pouring from its crooked chimney.

Ivan trembled with fear. Then he saw

the ant-sized cat grow to ladybird size
again. Then it grew to beetle size.

"I must be brave," said Ivan to
himself, and he stamped his foot hard,
and chased the cat into its own doorway.

A pile of snow slid from the cottage
roof and fell at Ivan's feet. He blinked
his eyes. The cottage had gone. The
witch had gone. The cat had gone. And
there, just in front of him was a
big log—and there was his own sledge,
green and red like the holly trees.

" Hullo ! Hullo ! " he called to his
friends.

" Hullo ! Hullo ! " came the answer
through the trees.

" I've got a fine log for Christmas,"
shouted Ivan, and he put it on his
sledge, and dragged it home over the
snow.

*Adapted by courtesy of
IPC Magazines*

A Wise Judge

One day a poor man found a bag
with a hundred silver coins in it.
He was very pleased.
Now he would be able to buy food
for his hungry children.

Then, that very day he heard
that a rich man in the town
had lost a bag of money
and would give a reward to the person
who brought it back to him.

At first the poor man thought,
" Shall I give the money back,
or shall I keep it ? The rich man
has plenty more riches,
but my poor children need food."
For a moment he was tempted
to keep the money. Then he thought,
" No, of course I mustn't keep it.
I will take it back at once."

He went to the rich man's house
and gave him the bag of money.
Now the rich man was mean and greedy,
and did not want to give a reward.

He hardly said thank you,
but straight away started
counting the money.

The poor man waited and waited.
Then he said quietly,
"I heard that you would give a reward."
"Reward!" said the rich man.
"You will get no reward.
You saw me count a hundred silver coins.
There were two hundred in the bag
when I lost it.
You must have stolen a hundred."

"I did not steal a single one,"
replied the poor man,
and he was so angry
that he took the rich man
to the judge.

The poor man told his story,
and the rich man told his.
When they had both finished,
the judge said to the rich man,
"How much money did you say
you had in the bag that you lost?"

" I had two hundred silver coins,"
said the rich man.
Then the judge said to the poor man,
" How much did you say
you found in the bag ? "
" One hundred silver coins," he replied.
Then the judge said to the rich man,
" If you lost two hundred silver coins,
this bag of money cannot be yours.
You must give it back
to the man who found it."

Adapted

Kiss a Pig

In Austria on New Year's Eve,
two things are supposed to be lucky.
One is to see a chimney sweep.
The other is to kiss a baby pig.

Lots of grown-up people go to parties
on that night, and sometimes
a chimney sweep takes a little pig
to the parties. The people crowd round
and try to kiss the little pig.

They must kiss it before midnight.
Then the new year will be a lucky one
for them.

Now in a village among the mountains
there lived a chimney sweep who had
two children. He had a girl called
Gretl and a boy called Peter.
On the last afternoon of the old year,
he said to them,

" Would you like to come to the farm
with me to fetch the new year pig ? "

" Yes, please," said Gretl and Peter.
The mountains and the fields lay deep
in snow, but the farm was not far, and
the farmer was waiting.

" Come and see mother pig and the family
first," he said. " They are in a pen in
the barn. December is not a good time
to have baby pigs, so I have to take
great care of them."

So Father, Gretl and Peter went into
the barn with the farmer. They leaned
over the wooden pen and looked at the
large mother pig lying in the straw.
She had nine little baby pigs with her.

They were three weeks old and they had
snub little noses and thin little tails.
Some were cuddled up asleep. Some were
lying about on top of each other,
and one was trying to climb over its
mother.

" Which is the new year pig ? "
asked Peter.

" Oh ! He's in another place. Can't
you hear him squeaking ? "

" Yes," said Gretl. " What's the matter
with him ? "

" He doesn't like being by himself,"
said the farmer. " Besides, I washed him
and scrubbed him all ready for you,
and he didn't like that at all."

He led them to the place where the new
year pig was lying on fresh, clean straw.

" Oh, isn't he sweet ? " said Gretl.

" And clean," added Peter.
It was the cleanest, pinkest baby pig
the children had ever seen.

The farmer lifted it out of its pen
and put it quickly into a basket with
a soft bit of blanket inside. The lid
of the basket was in two halves. He
fastened both parts down firmly. Then
he stroked the baby pig's cross little
face through a small, square hole
at one end.

" Be a good little pig," he said,
" and you'll be safely back with your
mother soon after midnight."

" I'll bring him back before I go
home," said the sweep.

" Yes. I'll be waiting to wish you
a happy new year," said the farmer.

Father, Gretl and Peter said goodbye,
and walked back along the path. Father
carried the basket, and the little pig
squeaked and grumbled all the way home.

" Now I must hurry away," said Father
to the children. " I have two more
chimneys to sweep this afternoon.
Look after the little pig and keep him

warm, and whatever you do,
keep the doors of the house closed."

" Yes, Father," said Gretl and Peter.
They took the basket into the house.
They showed the new year pig to Mother.
Then they took him out of the basket
and cuddled him and played with him.

The little pig squeaked and grumbled
at first. Then he began to get used to
the children, and he let them rub his
chest and stroke the top of his head.

" You must be very good tonight,"
said Peter to the pig. " Father will
take you to five parties, and you'll
have to let lots of people kiss you.
Then they will all have a happy new
year."

" I wish we could go to the parties,"
said Gretl. " But we shall be asleep in bed."

Mother had to go out that afternoon
but of course the children stayed at
home and played with the pig. The pig
was getting quite brave now. It was
sniffing round the chairs with its
little snub nose when there was a loud
bang at the door.

" That will be Max," said Peter.
" He's come to see the pig."
Peter jumped to his feet, rushed out of
the room, and opened the outside door
to his friend Max. He was in such a
hurry that he left the door of the room
wide open.

" The door ! " yelled Gretl, but it was

too late. The new year pig had darted
out and was gone.

Gretl, Peter and Max looked everywhere.
They did not know whether the little
pig had gone out of doors or not.
They looked in all the rooms downstairs.
They looked in all the rooms upstairs.
They looked up and down the street.

" He'll die of cold," wailed Gretl.

" And the village will lose its luck
for the whole year," said Max.

" And it's all my fault," added Peter,
nearly in tears.

Slowly the afternoon passed.
The children looked and looked
but they could not find the little pig.
They looked and looked
but they could not find the little pig.

" I'd better go home," said Max sadly
at last. He thought it might be a good
idea to go before the chimney sweep
came back. Max went. Peter closed the
door after him. Then he began to cry.

Soon Father came home. The children
heard him stamp the snow off his boots.

"Hullo," he called as he put on his
slippers in the kitchen. "How's Piggy?"
Gretl did not answer. Peter went on
crying.

Father went to the bathroom to have
a bath. He was very happy. The day's
work was done, and he was looking
forward to the parties and the fun.

He hoped the little pig would be good
and not wriggle in his arms too much.
He did not know, of course, that the
little pig was lost.

While Father was still in the bath,
Mother came back. She came into the
room where both the children were now
in tears.

" Whatever's the matter ? " she asked.

" We've lost the new year pig,"
they sobbed.

" Lost it ? " cried Mother. " Have you
looked for it ? "

" Yes."

" Have you looked everywhere ? "

" Yes. Everywhere."
Mother looked worried. She went out of
the room slowly, wondering where to
start looking first.

" I must say you left its basket in a
silly place," she said rather crossly.
" Right in the way, for everyone to fall
over."

She picked it up to move it.
It was heavy.
She raised one half of the lid. Then
she smiled.

"Here!" she called softly. "Gretl.
Peter."

The children came. They peeped in the
basket. There, cosy and warm inside,
lying on its bit of blanket, was the
tired little new year pig.

So everyone in the village had a happy new year after all; and the little pig was kissed and kissed and kissed.

Then, when midnight struck on the church clock, the chimney sweep took the little pig back to the farm.
He put it back in the pen with its mother and its brothers and sisters.
The little pig curled up beside them, warm and cosy.

It was New Year, but he did not know anything about that. He gave a soft little snort and fell asleep.

The Untidy Man

Mr Marmaduke Mortimer Dann
Is really a most untidy man,
With shaggy beard and tangled hair.
No wonder people turn and stare.

Wherever he goes, whatever he eats,
He drops his rubbish on the streets—
Bones and bits from his latest meal,
Paper bags and orange peel,

Empty boxes and battered tins,
Apple cores and banana skins.
Oh Mr Marmaduke Mortimer Dann
Is really a most untidy man !

The Golden Broom

Once upon a time, in a small cottage
in the country, there lived a mother and
a father and a little boy called Tangles.
They were rather poor, but they did not
worry about it, and they were very happy.

One winter night, when the sky was
black as velvet, and the air was filled
with snowflakes, there came a knock at
the door. This was very unusual because
the cottage was lonely and no one ever
called there after dark.

Mother opened the door a little way,
and Tangles stood behind her and peeped
round her skirts. There in the shadows
stood a man, and Tangles felt at once
that there was something strange about him.

"Good evening," said the man. "Could
you give me shelter for the night?
I have lost my way, and the snow is
growing deeper every moment."

Mother did not quite know what to do,
and she was about to say that there was
no spare bed in the cottage, when the
man walked in. He shut the door, and
said to Father,

" It's very kind of your wife to offer
me shelter for the night."

Father looked surprised,
for he had not heard Mother say a word.
He was just about to say that there was
no spare bed in the cottage, when
the man said,

" It's kind of you to offer me some
supper too."
Tangles opened his eyes as wide as
saucers, for he had not heard his father
say a word. The next moment, the man
looked at Tangles and said,

" And it's very kind of you to say that
you will give up your bed to me."

Tangles opened his mouth more widely
than his eyes, for he had not said
a word and he had not thought of
offering his bed to the stranger.

So the man stayed the night. He shared
the family's poor supper, and he curled
up in the little wooden bed that
belonged to Tangles. Tangles crept into

bed with his mother and father, and slept
till morning.

Next day the snow was white and deep,
but it was starting to melt and to drip
down from the roof and the window sills.
The man shared the family's poor
breakfast, and then sat by the window
watching the melting snow.

Father began to get ready to go to
work. Tangles began to get ready to go
to school. Mother began to sweep
the kitchen floor.

Suddenly the man stood up and said,

" Thank you for all your kindness to me.
Now I will repay you."

" No, no," replied Mother. " We do not
wish for payment."

" A present then," said the man. " I
will give you a present."
He looked round as if thinking
what to give. Then his eyes turned to
the broom in Mother's hands.

" That broom," he added. " May all the

dust it sweeps turn to gold."
Mother laughed.

" It's a kind thought," she said, but
Tangles thought it was not a proper
present at all.

Then the stranger smiled
and opened the door, and went out into
the snow.

" What a strange man," said Father, as
the footsteps died away.

" May all the dust it sweeps turn to
gold," laughed Mother. " As if it would !
Anyway it was a kind thought, and kind
thoughts matter more than money or gifts."

She turned round and began to sweep the dust from a corner of the kitchen. Tangles stood and watched for a moment, and his thoughts were far away.

Suddenly he saw something gleaming! The dust before the broom! It was turning to gold before his eyes!

" Sun's shining," said Mother as she went on sweeping. "Hurry up, Tangles. You'll be late for school."

" But the dust!" cried Tangles. " It's turning to gold! It's true! Look, Father!"

Father looked. Mother looked. Tangles looked. Yes, it was true. All the dust the broom swept was turning to gold.

" That broom," the man had said. " May all the dust it sweeps turn to gold."

That was just what was happening.

Father, Mother and Tangles stood and stared. Father picked up some of the

golden dust and let it run through his
fingers on to an empty plate. Each tiny
speck was hard and shining. It was real
gold.

" You'll both be late," said Mother
suddenly. " I'll sweep it all into a box.
You can look at it again tonight."
Father and Tangles put on their coats
and boots in a rush. They said goodbye
to Mother, and hurried away.
Father thought,
" I must have dreamed it."
Tangles thought,
" I must have dreamed it."

But at home in the cottage, Mother was
sweeping a little pile of gold dust into
a box, and day-dreaming about what she
would buy with it.

. . . . . .

Mother had always been a clean and tidy
person, and there was not really much
dust in the house. So she swept the
kitchen, the living room, the bathroom,
the bedroom. As she swept, the dust
turned to gold before her broom. She
put all the gold dust into the box.

Then she swept all the rooms again.
She went on sweeping, sweeping,
sweeping all day long until there was
not a speck of dust left in the house.
By the time Tangles came home from
school, and Father came home from work,
she was tired out.

On Saturday they walked into town and sold the gold dust. Then they bought new clothes and new shoes. They bought all sorts of nice things to eat.

They bought new blankets and new dishes. They bought new curtains and new chairs. They bought a new kettle and a bunch of early daffodils.

Then they went home feeling as happy as could be. It had been a happy day, but somehow no other day was as happy as that for a long, long time.

Father began to grumble at Mother for being clean and tidy.

" No wonder we can't find any more gold," he said. " You never let the house get dirty."

" Well, how can I find gold if I don't keep sweeping ? " she asked.

As for Tangles, he began to undo his good habits and turn them into bad habits. He stopped rubbing the mud off his boots when he came indoors. He stopped washing his hands.

He thought that if he brought a little extra dirt into the house, the dirt would turn to dust, and the dust would turn to gold before the broom.

Mother and Father became just as bad. Father tramped about the house in wellington boots. Mother even shook the door-mat inside the house instead of outside.

Then, almost as soon as they made the house dirty, they swept it clean again.

Father swept the floors.
Mother swept the floors.
Tangles swept the floors.
And as they swept, all the dust turned
to gold before the broom.

They did not really need any more
gold dust, and yet they went on sweeping
and sweeping, and trying to get more
and more and more. They seemed to be
working all day long, and by the time
spring came, they were all dirty and
untidy, and tired out with sweeping.
They were also cross and unhappy.

Then one day Tangles had an idea.

" Why not sweep out of doors ? " he
thought. " I'll climb up the hill, and
sweep the dry, dusty hillside."
So he climbed the hillside in front of
the cottage, and he began to sweep.

He swept and swept but he saw not a
speck of gold. In a way he felt glad.
He sat down to rest, and he began to
think. He was tired of sweeping, and

tired of gold dust too. He felt that
everything at home was all wrong.

He wished suddenly that he could burn
the broom, or break it or throw it
away. He remembered how happy Mother
and Father and he had been in the days
before dust had started turning into
gold. He wished everything could be as
it had been then.

The sun shone in his eyes and made him sleepy. He rolled over on his side and fell asleep, with the broom still in his hand.

When he awoke, he found he was holding nothing but a broken branch; and the broom was nowhere, nowhere to be seen.

．　．　．　．　．

Tangles thought his mother and father would be angry when he told them he had lost the broom. But they were not angry at all. In fact, they looked pleased.

" Perhaps it's a good thing," said Father.

" I'm glad," said Mother, and she went out and bought a new broom. It was just an ordinary broom, and it swept up ordinary dust that stayed just ordinary dust.

So everything began to feel right again. Mother, Father and Tangles became clean and tidy once more. They

rubbed their boots on the mat, and they
washed their hands. They had time to
talk to each other and read to each
other and play games together.

They were all happy again, and except
for the new things they had bought,
everything seemed just as it had been in
the beginning.

But not quite everything.

On the bare hillside in front of the
cottage windows, something began to
grow. It was a dainty, green bush, and
it was covered with yellow flowers.

Year by year it grew bigger and
stronger, till all the hillside was
covered with yellow blossoms, and when
the sun shone on them, they sparkled
like gold.

"How beautiful they are," said Mother
and Father and Tangles to each other.
And the flowers, though you may not
believe it, were called "broom".

An Egg

Who can describe the shape of an egg?
Not oval, not round,
Never square.
Not pointed, not flat,
Not this shape, nor that,
A shape you don't see anywhere,
Except
In an egg.

Petra and the Goat

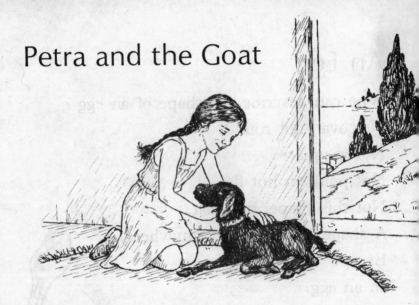

There was once a little Greek girl
whose name was Petra. She lived on an
island that rose steeply out of the blue,
blue sea. Her house was small and white
like all the other houses, but it was at
the very top of the dusty path that led
up from the shore.

Now Petra had a goat called Luki.
Luki was black as night, and his ears
flopped down on each side of his face
like bits of soft velvet. He wore a blue
and red collar that Petra's mother had
made for him.

Petra loved Luki, and Luki usually followed her everywhere. But this morning Luki was missing. Where could he be ?

Petra looked inside the house. Luki was not there. She looked outside the house. Luki was not there. She looked down the path. She looked among the rocks and the olive trees, but Luki the goat was nowhere to be found.

" Don't worry," said Mother to Petra. " He'll come back soon." So Petra tried not to worry. She went to the place that she called her " look-out " and she climbed up on to a flat rock. She gazed down at the sea and the ships and the harbour.

There was always something to watch, for ships called at the island every day in the summer. They brought people with bundles and baskets, and boxes of things to sell.

They brought people who were on holiday. Some people stayed a night in the small hotel near the shore, and then caught another boat next day, and went on to another island.

There was a ship in the harbour now. Petra could see people walking, one by one, along the gangway. She could see them stepping off the gangway on to the island.

But what was that, going in and out among the people ? What was that, pushing its nose into their baskets ?

It was a black goat, and though it looked so small and far away, Petra was sure it was Luki.

Petra ran and scrambled down the hillside. She had her own short cuts among the trees and rocks. Down, down, down she went until she came to the harbour.

Now, where was Luki ? Petra could not see him at first. Then she saw three people sitting on a seat, sharing their picnic lunch with a goat. They were

laughing and talking, and feeding him
with rolls and butter.

The goat, of course, was Luki! He was
as black as night, and his ears flopped
down on each side of his face like bits
of soft velvet. He wore the blue and red
collar that Petra's mother had made for
him. It was Luki all right!

" Luki! Luki! " called Petra. Luki
gave a last sniff in the picnic bag, and
then came walking over to her.

The two of them climbed and scrambled
up the hillside. They used their own
short cuts among the trees and rocks
until they reached home once more.
Petra was very glad to have Luki back.

" You mustn't go down to the harbour
again," she told him.

But Luki did go. He went again the
very next morning, and Petra went down
later, in the hot sun, to look for him.
There was Luki, meeting the people from
a boat. There he was, pushing his nose

into their baskets, taking titbits from their hands, or sharing their picnics.

Soon the goat was going down to the harbour every day. People seemed to like him. They stroked him and patted him and fed him. The sailors and the fishermen and the boatmen all began to know him. They began to know the goat with his black, black coat and his floppy ears and his blue and red collar.

Luki began to stay down there all day, and to come home only in the evening. Petra felt very unhappy about it. Luki did not want to follow her about as he had done before. He seemed to think only of rushing away down to the harbour.

There was nothing Petra could do to stop him, unless she were to tie him up all day, and she did not want to do that.

" Never mind," said Mother sometimes. " Luki is a young goat. Perhaps he will get tired of the harbour soon, and settle down again at home."

But Luki did not get tired of the harbour. He went down there every morning and stayed all day. Then, in the evening he came home.

Then one evening he did *not* come home! Where was he now?

" He'll come home before it gets dark," said Mother, but he did not. Petra sat up and waited for him. She waited and waited but Luki did not come.

" I'll look for him," said Father, and he went down the dusty path with a lantern. Father often went down to the harbour in the evenings and talked to his friends. Someone might be able to tell him where to find Luki the goat.

But when Father came home later, and found Petra still awake, he said,

" No one has seen Luki this evening.
I think he might have walked on to
a ship. Some of the men were telling me
that Luki is always on the gangway
meeting everyone. He could easily have
walked on to a ship."

"A ship!" said Petra. "Some of
those ships call here only once a week!"

"Well, at least everyone knows him,"
said Father. "He'll come back safely,
sooner or later. Don't worry, Petra."

But Petra did worry. She worried
till she fell asleep. Then she worried
again in the morning when she woke up.

When afternoon came, she worried even
more, for the sky grew dark, and a storm
blew up with sudden fury. The wind cut
across the island like a knife, and the
sea was tossed into clouds of white foam.
Thunder crackled and rumbled. Flashes of
lightning seemed to tear the sky apart.

Petra was very, very worried. Was
Luki on a ship in *this*?

When evening came, it was calm and beautiful. The storm had worn itself out, and blown itself away. The sea was quiet and the air was still.

" Come down to the harbour with me," said Father kindly to Petra. "You've been indoors all the afternoon. There may be a ship for us to meet."

" There are none due tonight," replied Petra. She knew the names of all the ships, and she knew when they were all due to call.

" But the *Island Queen* isn't in yet," said Father. " It's very late because of the storm. It may still come before sunset."

The *Island Queen* was a small ship that sailed between some of the islands, and called every day.

" Do you think Luki might be on the *Island Queen* ? " asked Petra hopefully.

" He might. You never know," replied Father.

So Father and Petra walked down to the harbour. There were quite a lot of people there, waiting for the *Island Queen*.

" She'll be coming in about half an hour," someone told Father. " But she won't be able to leave again tonight."

Soon the ship came in. The ropes were thrown ashore and made fast to the harbour. There was all the usual noise and chatter as people walked down the gangway, and other people met them.

" What a storm ! " everyone was saying. " What a storm ! "

Down the gangway they came, men, women and children, with baskets and bundles and boxes.

Eagerly, hopefully, Petra gazed at them all. Eagerly, hopefully, she waited for a black goat called Luki.

All the people hurried down the gangway, and stepped ashore. There were men, women and children, but there was no goat.

One more man came, then no one else.
No goat.

Petra turned her face away because
she was nearly in tears.

"Petra!" cried Father. "Look!"
A sailor was stepping down the gangway,
leading a goat by a piece of rope. The
goat was as black as night, and his ears
flopped down on each side of his face
like bits of soft velvet. He wore a blue
and red collar. It was Luki!

" Luki ! " cried Petra. " Luki ! "
She put her arms round Luki's neck, and
hugged him. As for Luki, he rubbed his
cold nose against Petra, as if trying to
say how pleased he was to be back.

" Is it your goat ? " asked the sailor.

" Yes," replied Petra.

" No one knew he was on the boat
yesterday until we were out at sea,"
explained the sailor. " Then today, in
the storm, he felt very sorry for
himself. He'll never make a good sailor.
In fact I don't think he'll try going on
a ship again."

And Luki didn't. He had been very
frightened by the storm and the tossing
of the ship. All he wanted now was to
stay safely at home with Petra.

So after that, he played with Petra
among the rocks and trees, or lay down
in the sun at the door, and he never,
never went down to the harbour again.

Running and Shouting

I'm running because
   I am wanting to run.
I'm not in a hurry.
   I'm running for fun.
I'm crossing a field
   and I'll run down the hill
And I'll run by the stream
   that can never keep still.
I'll run in the rain
   and I'll run in the sun.
I'll run and I'll run
   and I'll run and I'll run!

I'm shouting because
  I am wanting to shout.
It's a nice sort of noise
  and there's no one about.
I'm crossing the field
  and I'll shout down the hill
And I'll shout by the stream
  that can never keep still.
I'll shout in the rain
  and I'll shout in the sun.
I'll run as I shout
  and I'll shout as I run!

The Station Party

There were five children living in
Railway Cottages.
David and Nicky lived in number one.
Penny and Andrew lived in number two.
Paula lived in number three.

Some of them remembered that when they
were little they had climbed on their fences
and watched the trains go past.

There were no trains now.
Grass and brambles had crept over the
track. The station had not been used for
years. Cobwebs hung at the windows.
Stuffing was bursting out of the long,
padded seat in the waiting room.

The lock on the door had rusted in the rain, and the door swung to and fro with every wind that blew.

One winter, a few days after Christmas, Paula said,

" Let's have a party in the station waiting room."

" Good idea," agreed the others.

" We'll ask our mothers for food."

" And we'll put up some paper chains to cheer the place up a bit."

" When shall we have it ? "

" Wednesday. We'll have it early in the afternoon so that we get home before dark. Two o'clock till four o'clock ? "

" Yes."
So the plans were made.

The station was about ten minutes' walk away from Railway Cottages, and more than half an hour's walk from the village. Even in its busy days, it had always been rather a quiet, lonely little station.

On Wednesday the children walked along

together, just before two o'clock.
David and Nicky carried a tin of
sandwiches and a bag of paper chains.

Penny and Andrew carried some mince
pies and little iced cakes.

Paula carried chocolate biscuits,
a bottle of lemonade
and a bunch of holly.

David pushed open the creaking door,
and Nicky put a stone against it to keep
it shut.

Paula put the bunch of holly
in the fireplace. It was a cold day, and
the wind whistled down the chimney and
rustled the stiff leaves.

The boys pinned the paper chains above
the windows, and Penny spread a paper
tablecloth over the padded seat.

The children played games and ran races
on the shaky floor. They laughed and
shouted and told jokes and asked riddles.
They had their tea and then played again.

The afternoon passed very quickly, and
suddenly someone cried in surprise,

" It's getting dark already."

Andrew folded up the paper tablecloth,
and Paula gathered up the food that was
left over. There were three sandwiches,
two mince pies, two little iced cakes
and a few chocolate biscuits.

" I'll put them all in the tin till we
get home," she said.

" It's snowing," said David. He was

trying to unpin the paper chains, but he could not get the first pin out.

" I think we'd better leave everything, and come and clear up in the morning," said Penny. " We promised to be home before dark."

" Just take the food then."

They were excited by the snow, and in the scramble to hurry home, even the tin of food was left behind. They pushed the creaking door shut, and Andrew put the stone against it. They laughed and ran along the country road to Railway Cottages.

For two hours, the old station had come to life again. Now it was lonely and silent once more, except for the wind whistling down the chimney, and the paper chains shivering in the windows.

That same evening, after the children had all arrived home, a tramp went walking across the fields. It was almost dark but he knew exactly where he

was going. He was going to the old
station.

In the summer he always slept out of
doors under the stars. He slept against
a hedge or just inside a gate. But in
winter when it was cold and wet and
windy, he liked a warmer bed. He liked
to find an old hut or a barn or a
country bus shelter.

He had slept at the old station many
times before. He knew no one would
worry him there, and he would be out of
the way of the wind and the falling snow.

He came to the station and pushed open
the waiting room door. Ah! There was
the long padded seat. It was one of the
best beds he had in all the year.

The last of the pale daylight lit up
the lonely room. The tramp looked round
in surprise. There were gay paper chains
hanging among the cobwebs. There was a
bunch of holly in the grate.

Someone must have been expecting him.
Some kind person had tried to make him
feel welcome. Then he noticed the tin
on the seat. He opened it. Someone had
even left some supper for him!

" Mince pies ! " he said to himself.
" Sandwiches. Cakes. I haven't had such
a feast for years ! " A wave of happiness
went through him, and he sat down and
began to eat.

When he had finished, he curled up on
the seat and pulled his ragged coat round
his knees. The waiting room was very
cold, but to him it was a palace.

He thought for a long while before he
went to sleep. He was a strange man.
He wandered the roads year in, year out,
because he did not like the world of
people and machines.

Machines were ugly and noisy. They
drowned all the small, sweet sounds of
nature. People were greedy and unkind.

But tonight he began to wonder if he were wrong after all. Here was such kindness from a stranger. Here were paper chains and holly to welcome him. Here was food for him to eat. The tramp sighed and fell asleep.

The paper chains swayed a little, and the holly leaves crackled in the grate. Outside, snow went whirling across the fields in misty clouds.

. . . . . .

The children ran to the station early the next morning. The tramp, because of the snow, was rather late leaving.

David pushed the door. It seemed to be stuck at first. Then it opened suddenly so that the children half tumbled into the room. It was hard to tell who was the more surprised, the tramp or the children.

For a moment they all stared at each other. Then the tramp said,

" I think you must be the kind people
who left my supper here last night."

" Supper ? " said Andrew.

" The supper in the tin. It was the
best I've had for months. And the room
looked so pretty with the paper chains
and holly."

Nicky was about to explain that the
things were left over from the party,
but Paula said quickly,

" We're glad you liked it."
She would like to have talked to the
tramp. She wanted to ask him *why* he was

a tramp. Why was *anyone* a tramp?
But the tramp stood up and said,

" Thank you. Thank you all very much
indeed." Then he went out of the door
and walked through the snow to the open
road. The children watched him till he
was out of sight.

Then Penny said slowly,

" It was a good party, and I'm glad
the tramp had a share in it."

Moles

It must be dull for little moles
Making tunnels, digging holes.
What can they hear down in the dark ?
A blackbird's song ? A fox's bark ?

Or only the sighing of roots down below,
And the whisper of seeds
                      that are waiting to grow ?

Worm Treasures

A little worm is working hard
Underneath the ground,
Saying to his nearby friends,
   " See what I have found !—
A little bit of crumpled leaf,
A root that's running deep,
A treasure hoard of daffodils
Locked in their bulbs asleep."

Salty the Pigeon

Salty was a pigeon whose home was in the
north of England. One day he was set
free in France. It was July the ninth.
He started to fly towards home but he
met strong winds.

He tried hard to fly against them,
but he was blown further and further out
of his way.

On July the twenty-fourth some sailors
found him lying on the deck of their
ship. The ship was on its way to Canada.

Salty was tired out, but the sailors looked after him, and he soon felt better. When the ship reached Canada, Salty was given to a man who kept pigeons. This man looked at the tiny band on Salty's leg, and read his number. Then he was able to find out where Salty lived.

He put Salty in a cage and tied a label to it. The label said,

"Very Important Pigeon."

Salty was put on to an aeroplane, a British Airways VC-10, and flown to his own home.

The Eagle and the Shoe

Long, long ago in Egypt, an eagle flew
down over a lady's house. It picked up
one of her shoes and carried it away.
Later, the eagle dropped it in the lap
of the King of Egypt. The King thought
it was such a dainty shoe, that he
wanted to find out who owned it.
He asked that the lady whose shoe
it was, should come to his court.
Soon she came, and the King married her.

Perhaps this was what gave someone
the idea for the story of Cinderella.